# Antoinette and the Story of the Jellyfish Monster

Written by Alison McGregor
Illustrated by Arielle Shira

One fine day in Jamaica long ago
-a time just out of reach-
young Antoinette Barbour walked
with her parents to the beach.

Antoinette was so excited she was marching
three steps ahead of everyone.
Mrs. Barbour began to scold her
as she was upset she now had to run.

"Antoinette you are too much.
young ladies should never rush."

So she slowly walked on her tippy
toes to make her seem older;
to make her look tall.

But this did not make Mrs. Barbour
happy. No, not at all.

Mr. Barbour sat Antoinette down and said scratching his stubble,
"Don't swim too far out, follow the rules
and DO NOT GET INTO ANY TROUBLE."

She promised her very best promise to be on her very best behaviour.
She would be a fine young lady, she swore. She would not waiver.

As soon as they left, she darted to the water,
forgetting immediately that she was to be a polite young daughter.

As she waited for the waves to cool
her off from the hot, hot day
she noticed a diving platform a
short distance away.

All she wanted was to do
the **biggest** cannonball
the beach had ever seen.

Everyone would cheer
and dance for the coolest little
girl that had ever been.

She climbed up onto the platform planning
her **greatest** cannonball of all time
when she bumped right into an older boy's behind.

"Watch it!" he grumbled to little Antoinette.
It was then she saw the longest lineup to jump
and with a sinking heart began to fret.

This was the longest line she ever had to wait in, she thought.
Each diver took so much time to jump,
leaving her completely distraught.

Antoinette furrowed her brow.
She simply had to do the world's greatest
cannonball. She had to do it RIGHT NOW!

She had to be **smart**. She needed a plan.
So, she looked up at the line again.

No one was on the left;
they were all to the right.
Her brain began to click and tick.
Then things began to look bright.

She needed to **focus**.
She needed to concentrate.
To the left side she would run
to make this jump oh-so great.

She flew past the line in a **flash**. Soon her dreams would come true.
But she could not hear what people were yelling. She didn't have a clue.

She took a great leap, curled her body up into the perfect ball
and braced herself for the big, fantastic fall.

She took a quick peek before her most **splendid** splash,
when she first spotted them flitting past in a flash.

Dozens of them. Plump and lumpy. Shiny and brilliant. JELLYFISH!
They seemed to reach out to her with their tentacles
wanting to eat her like a nice roast beef dish.

They surrounded her like lightning, moving so quickly.
They slapped her and stung her until she began to feel quite sickly.

She could not remember what happened next
but before she knew it, she was back on the
platform feeling quite perplexed.

She looked down
at her arms and legs
which began to welt,
ache and swell.
She looked at the
lifeguard beside her
who seemed very angry.
But why, she could
not tell.

He pointed over his shoulder to a sign that read,
"DANGER: Stinging jellyfish ahead".

The lifeguard whistled for a boat
to pick them both up.
Once ashore he said, "Don't worry we'll
take care of you little pup."

Now came the time for Mr. and Mrs. Barbour to return from town.
They looked up and down the beach but there was no Antoinette to be found.

Mr. Barbour shouted in a voice most stern
"Antoinette you come out this very instant you wee bairn."

Mrs. Barbour then took off with an ear-piercing scream.
"It's a monster!" she cried and ran away from a sight most mean.

A pinkish blob appeared from the shade of a palm tree.
The closer it came Mr. Barbour swore he heard, "tee hee!"

It had brownish spots here and there
and long seaweed **tentacles**.

A strange shaped mass with a funny walk;
it was quite the spectacle.

Now the whole beach was
in such a **commotion**.

**But then**
Mr. Barbour noticed
he could smell
calamine lotion.

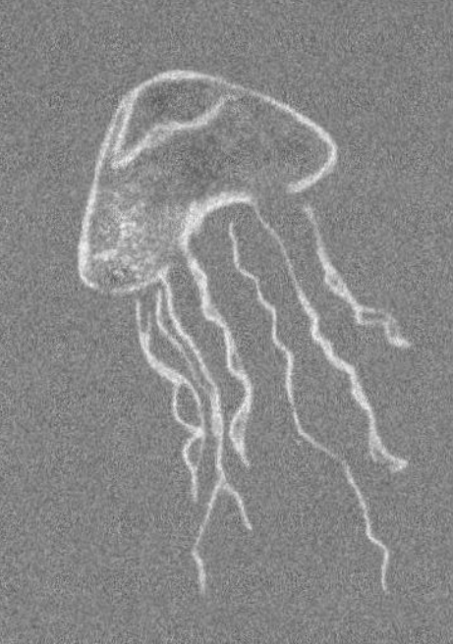

"Antoinette!" he exclaimed as the monster slowly came closer. He peeled back a layer of kelp to see his sore little girl; eyes lowered.

**(Apparently, long ago the only cure for jellyfish stings was to dress up as the same sort of thing.)**

Mr. Barbour gave a tsk tsk while trying to hide his laugh just a little bit.

Then they went to find Mrs. Barbour who was still sounding bonkers screaming and yelling of jellyfish monsters.

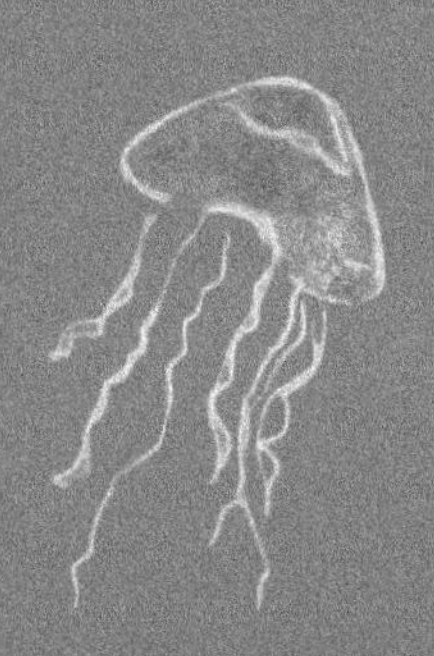

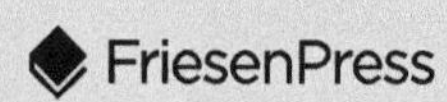

Suite 300 - 990 Fort St
Victoria, BC, V8V 3K2
Canada

www.friesenpress.com


First Edition — 2021

Illustrated by Arielle Shira



ISBN
978-1-5255-8709-2 (Hardcover)
978-1-5255-8710-8 (Paperback)
978-1-5255-8711-5 (eBook)

*1. JUVENILE FICTION, STORIES IN VERSE*

Distributed to the trade by The Ingram Book Company

CPSIA information can be obtained
at www.ICGtesting.com
Printed in the USA
BVHW020525200421
605002BV00002B/24